I0783666

COMRADES

Dale Lazarov & Enrique Nieto

COMRADES

StickyGraphicNovels.com

Printed and distributed by
ComicMix, LLC.,
71 Hauxhurst Ave. Suite B
Weehawken, NJ 07086.
http://www.comicmix.com

Hardcover ISBN: 9781939888648

AIGUO
爱国

AIGUO
爱国

AIGUO
愛國

HOTEL KOSMOS

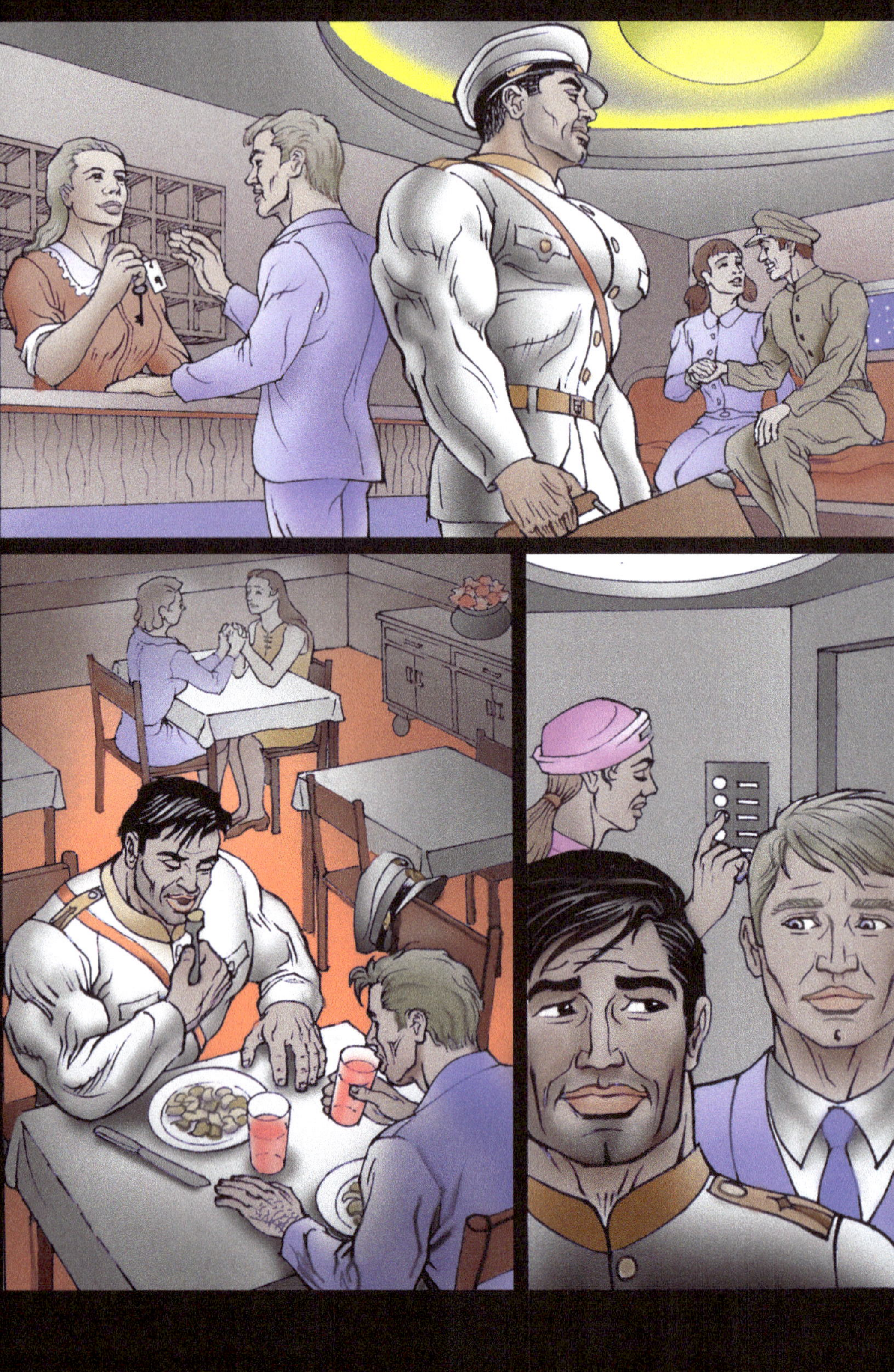

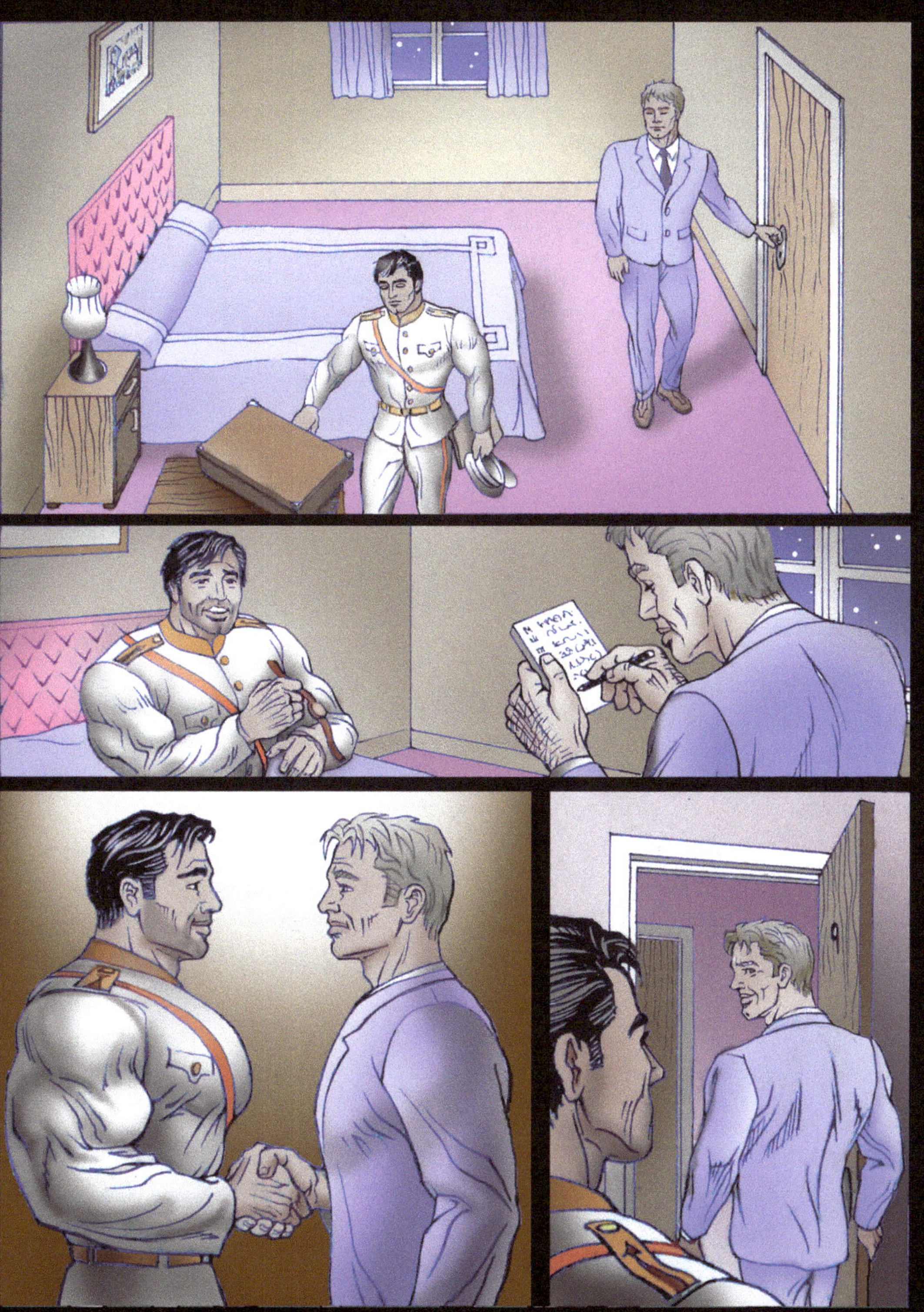

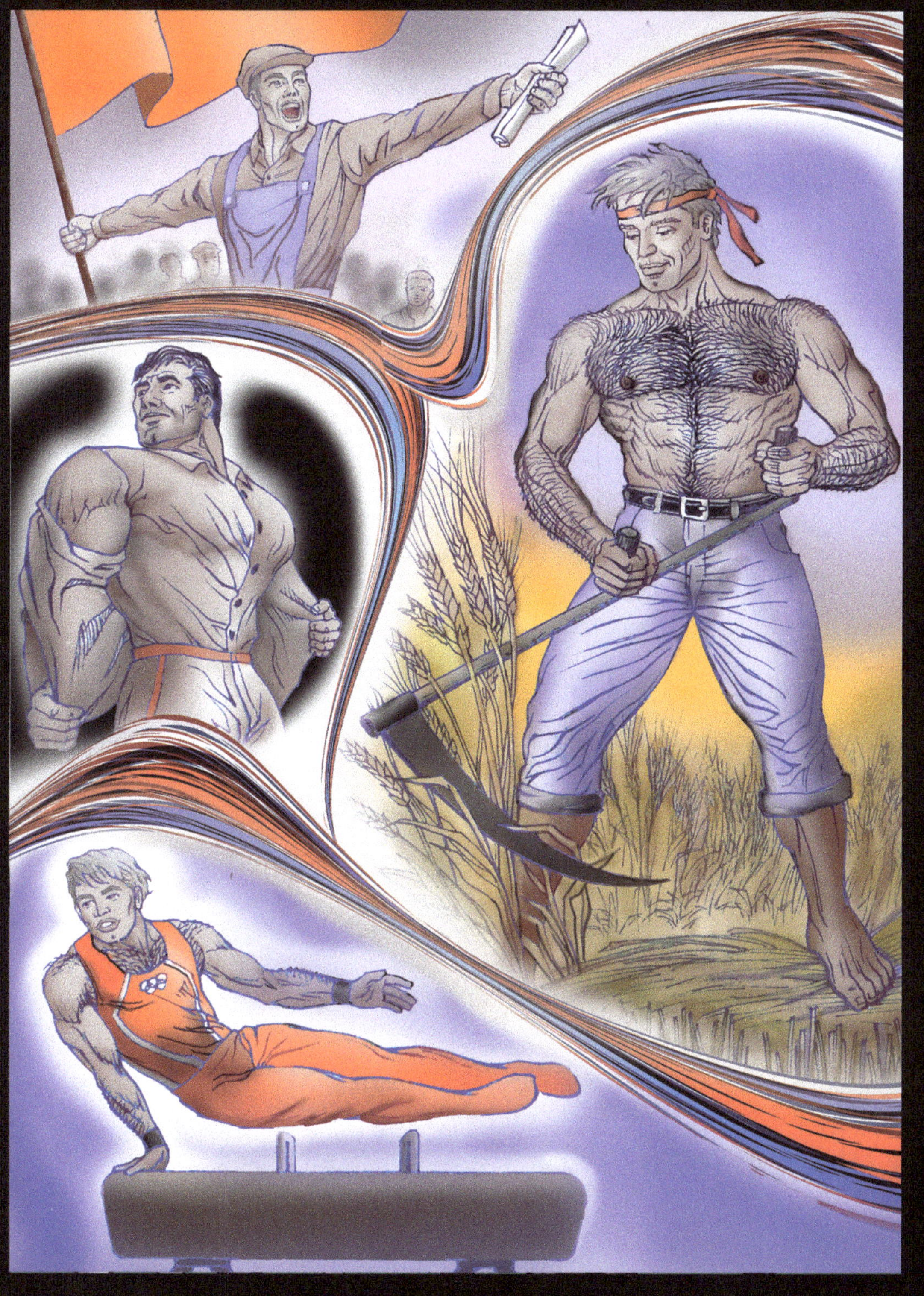

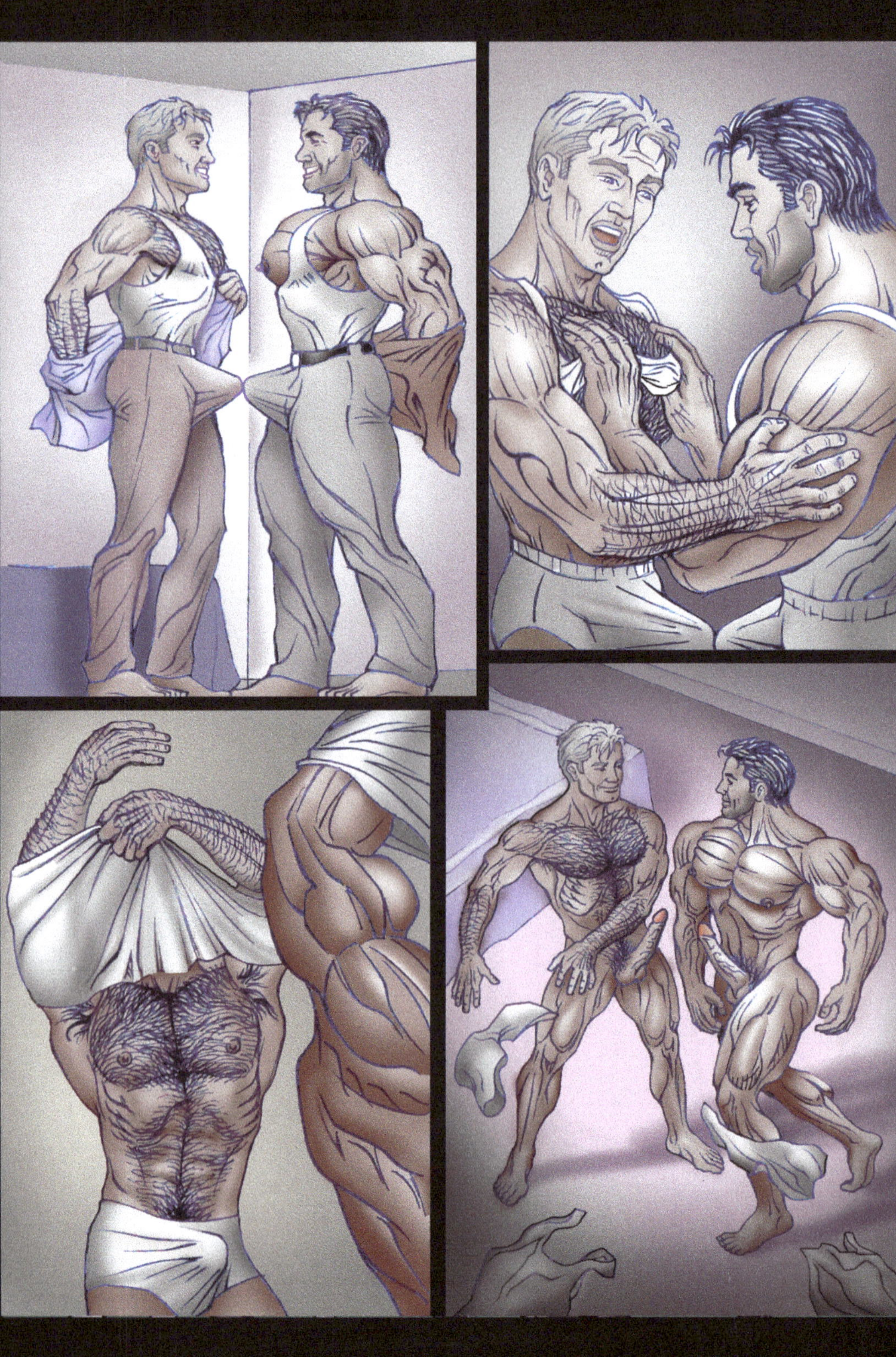

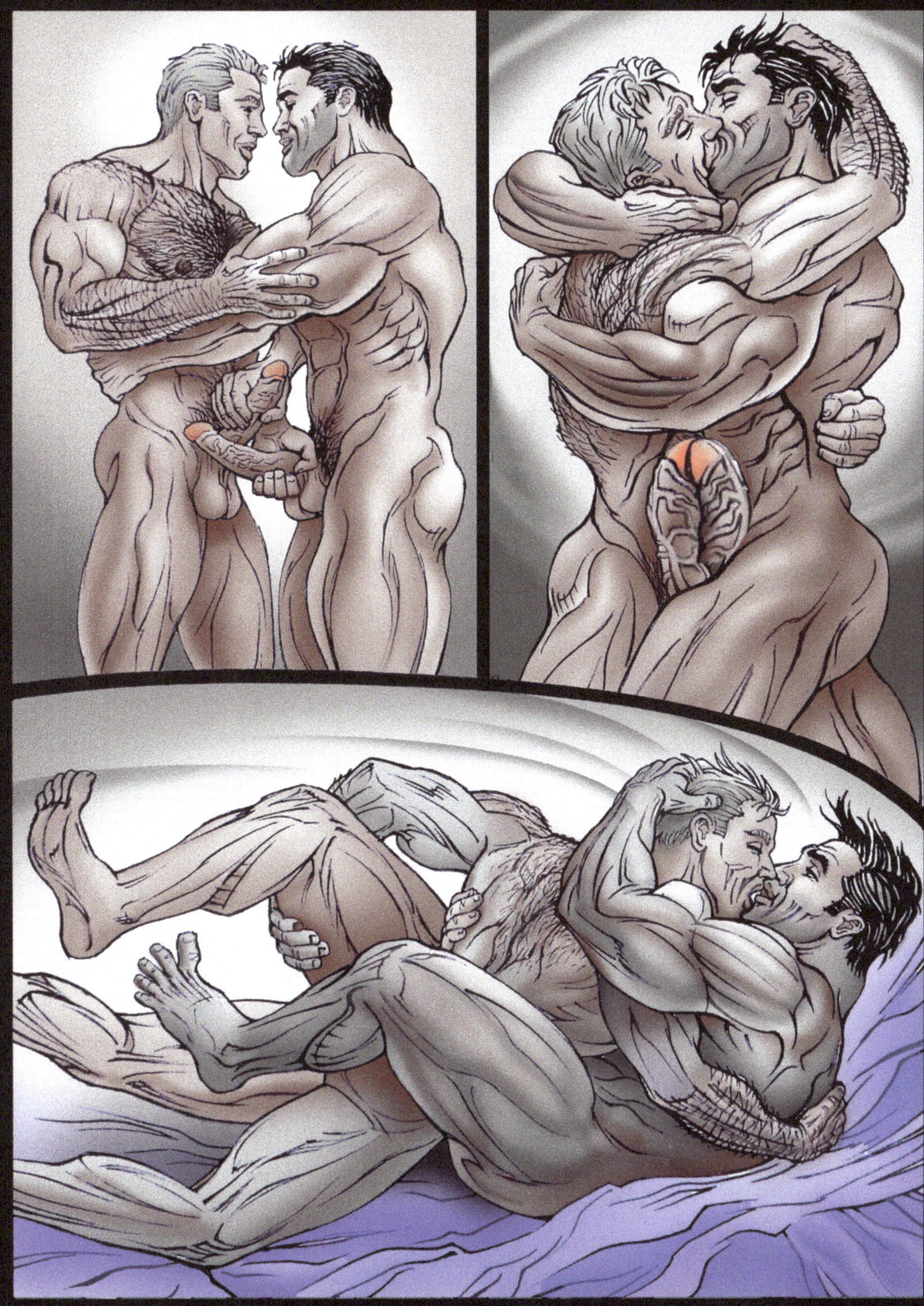

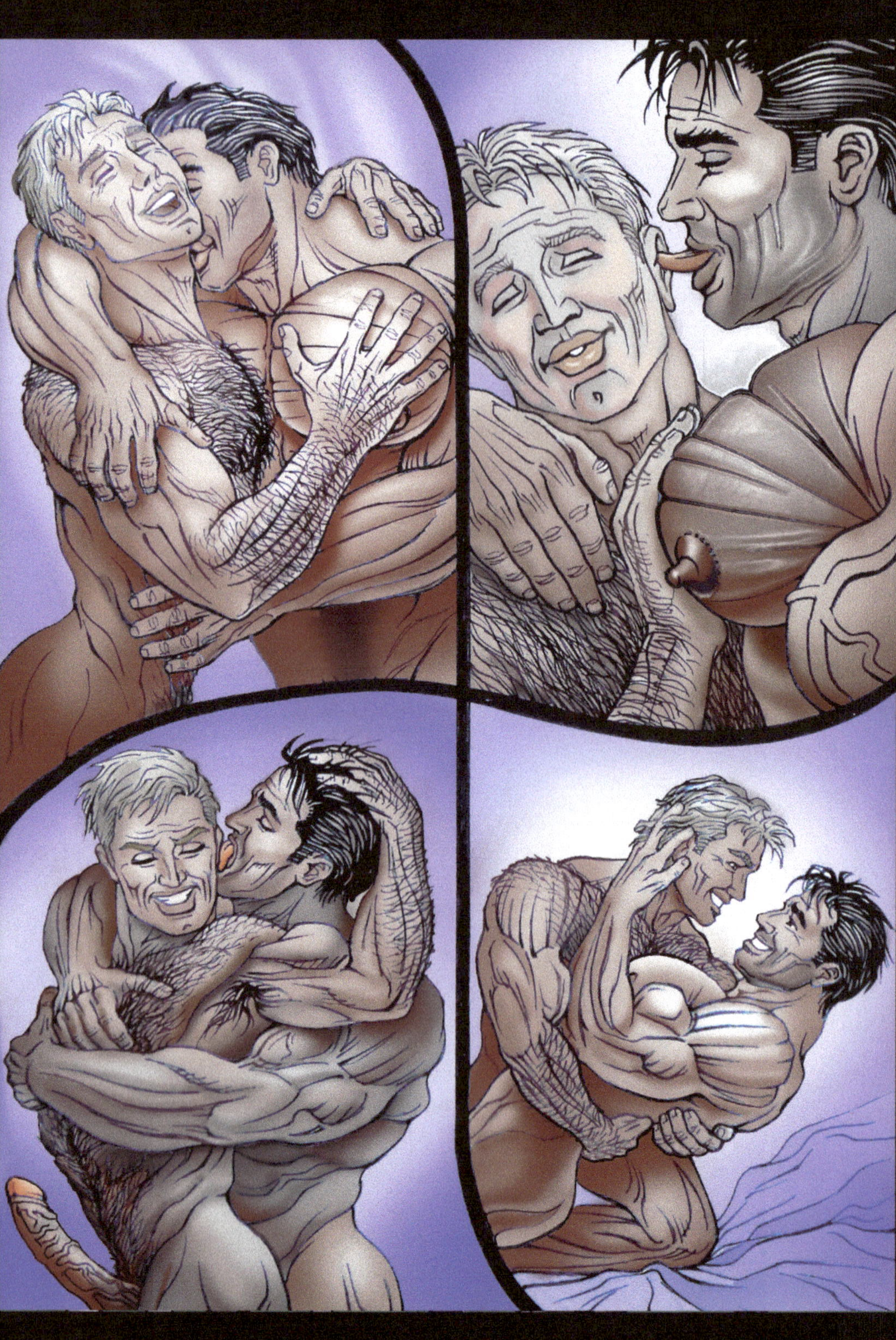

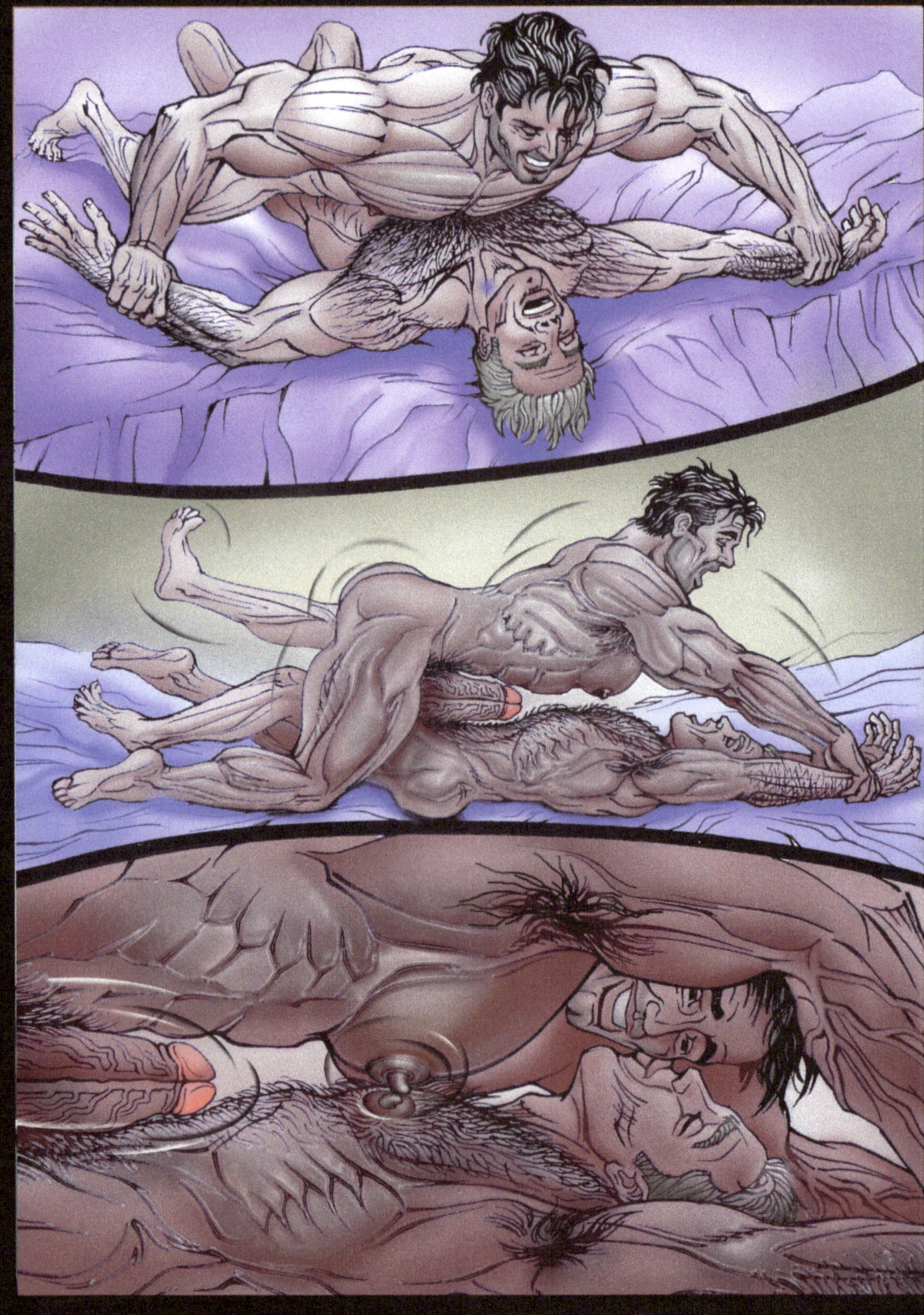

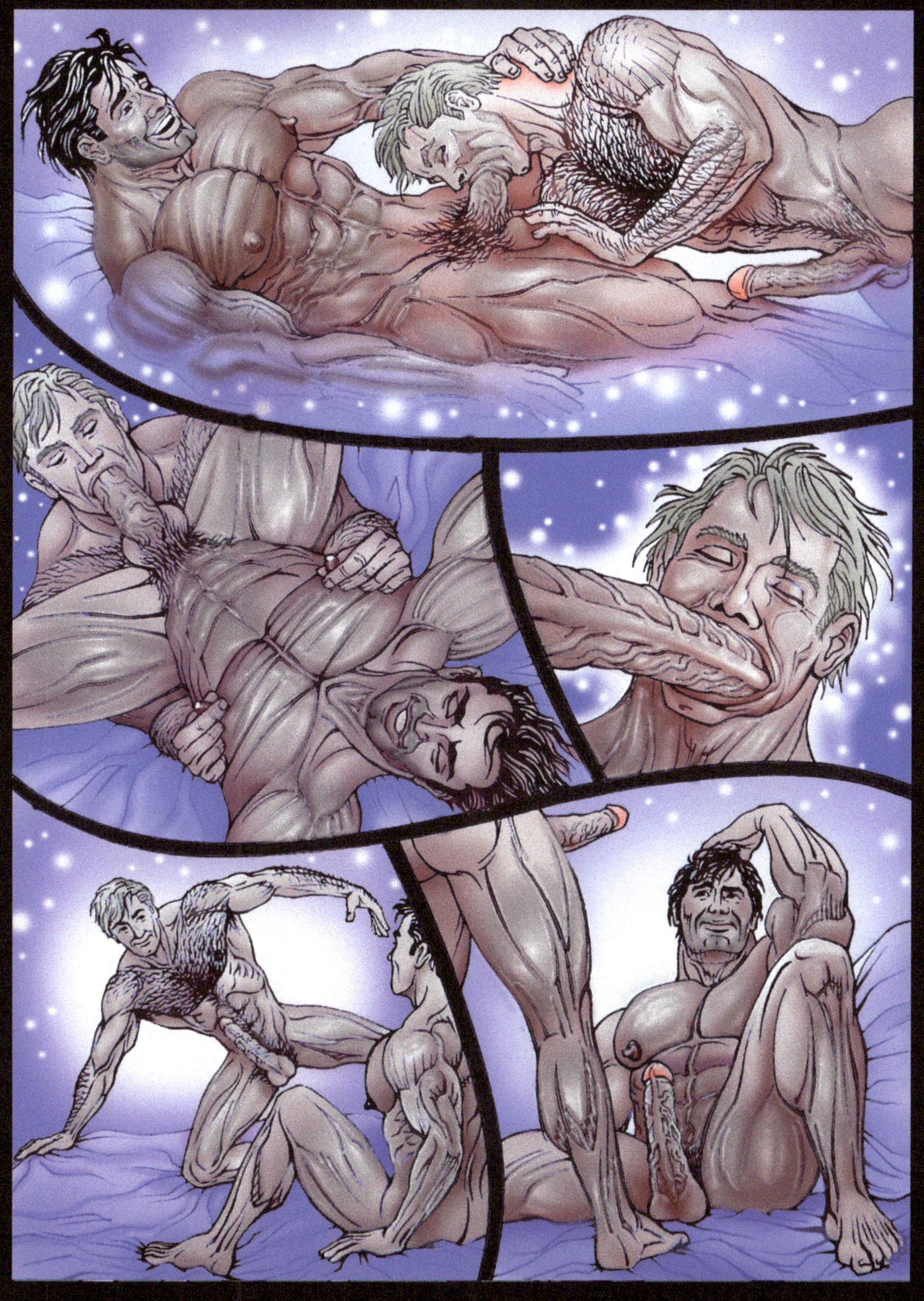

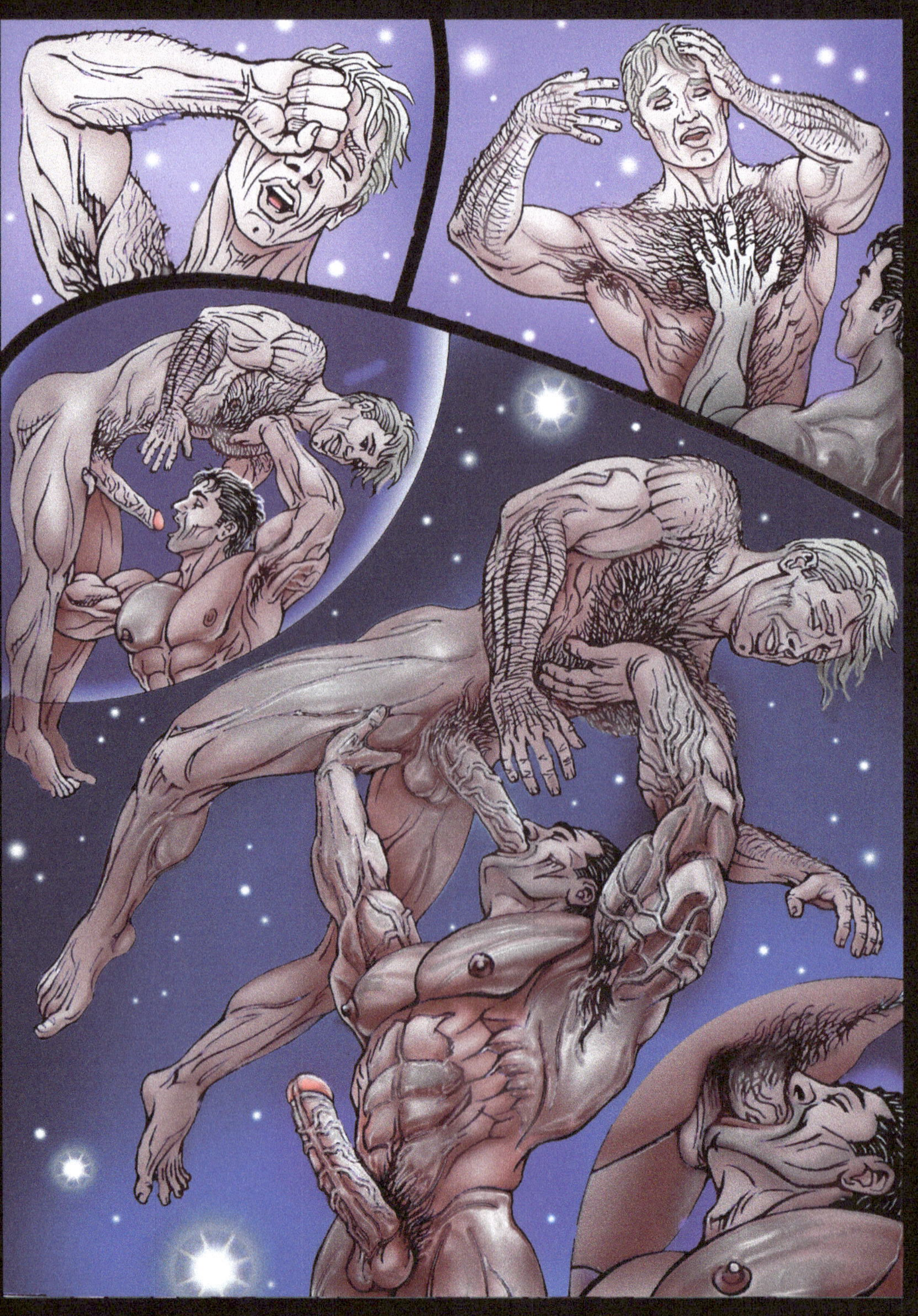

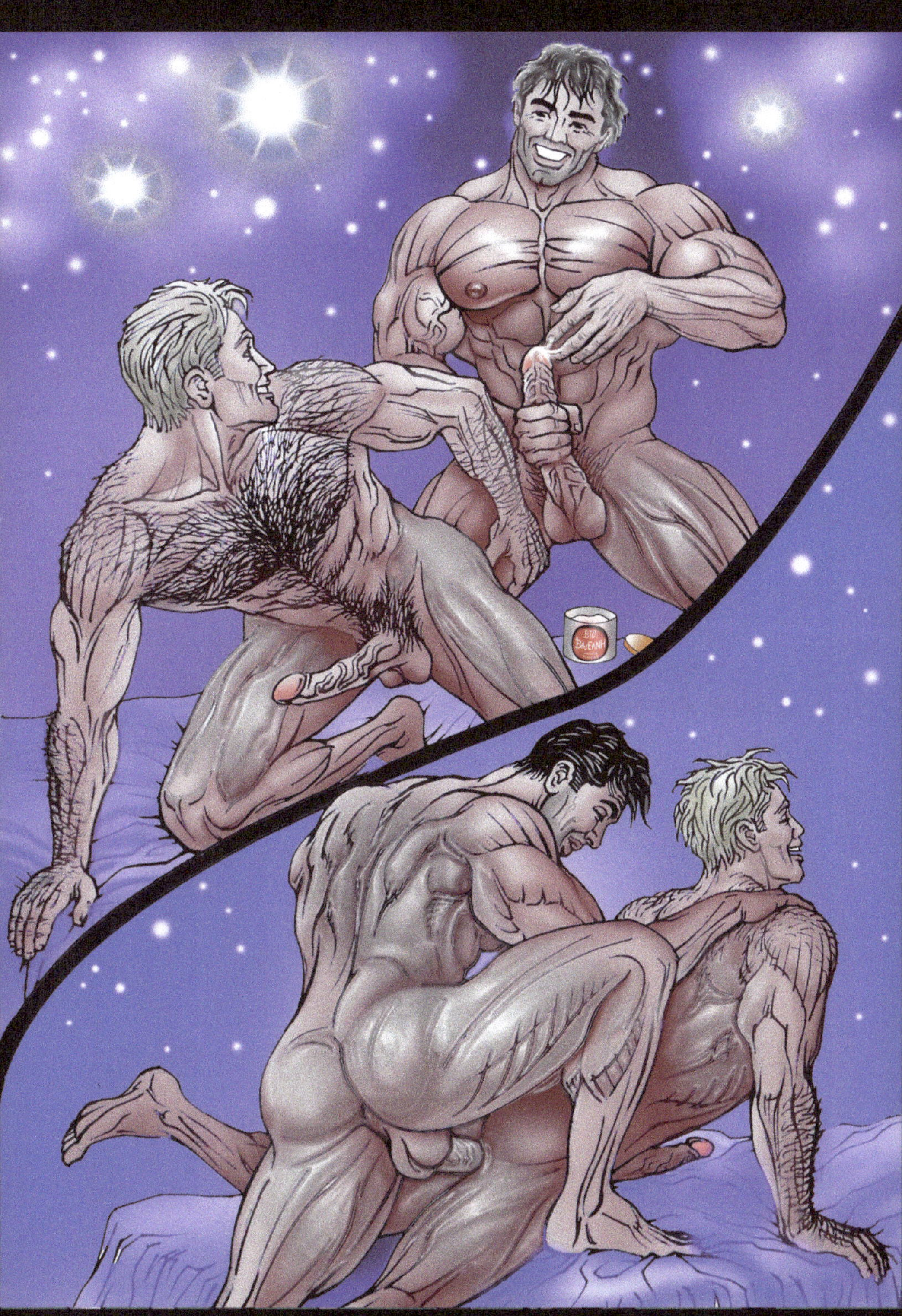

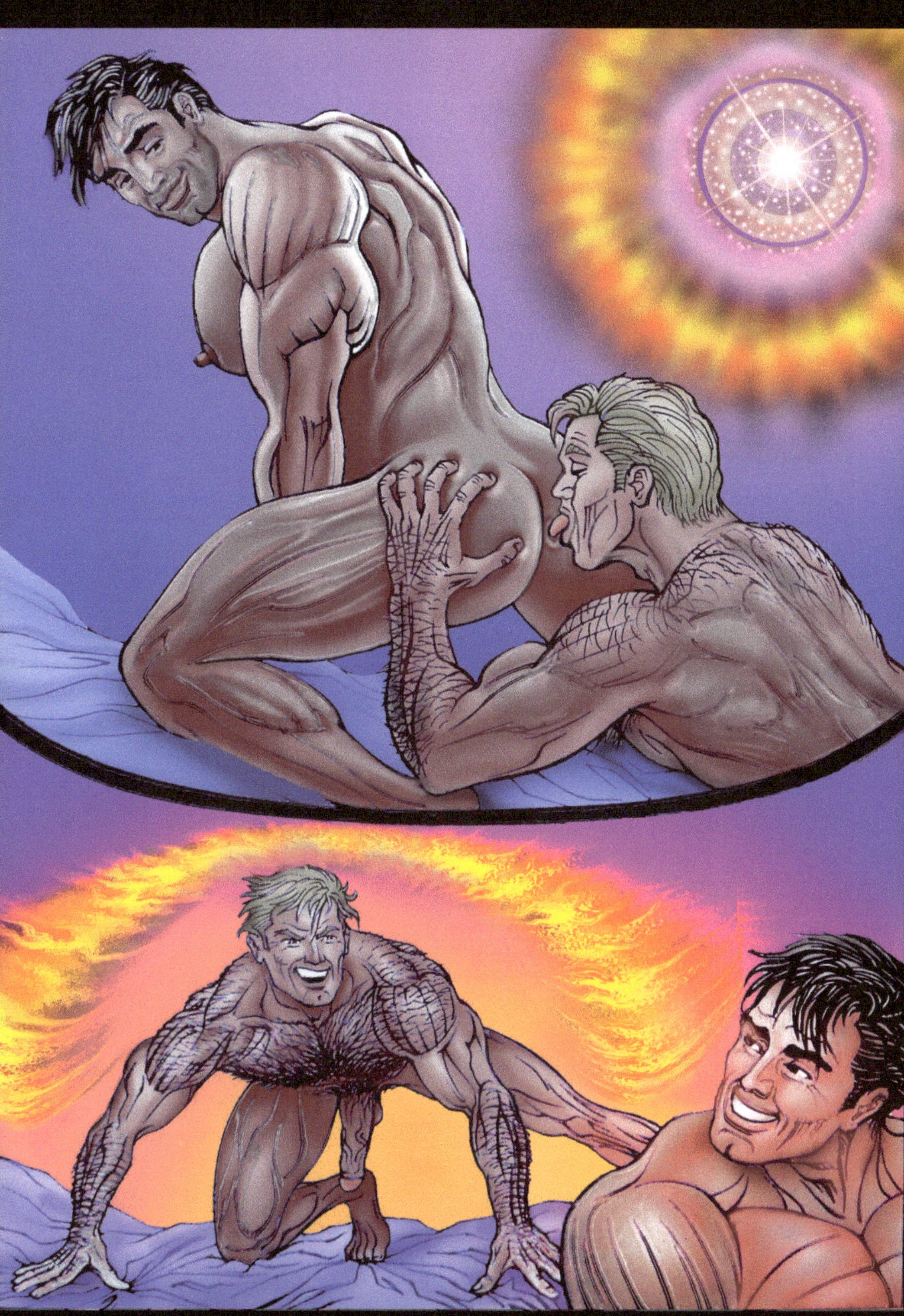

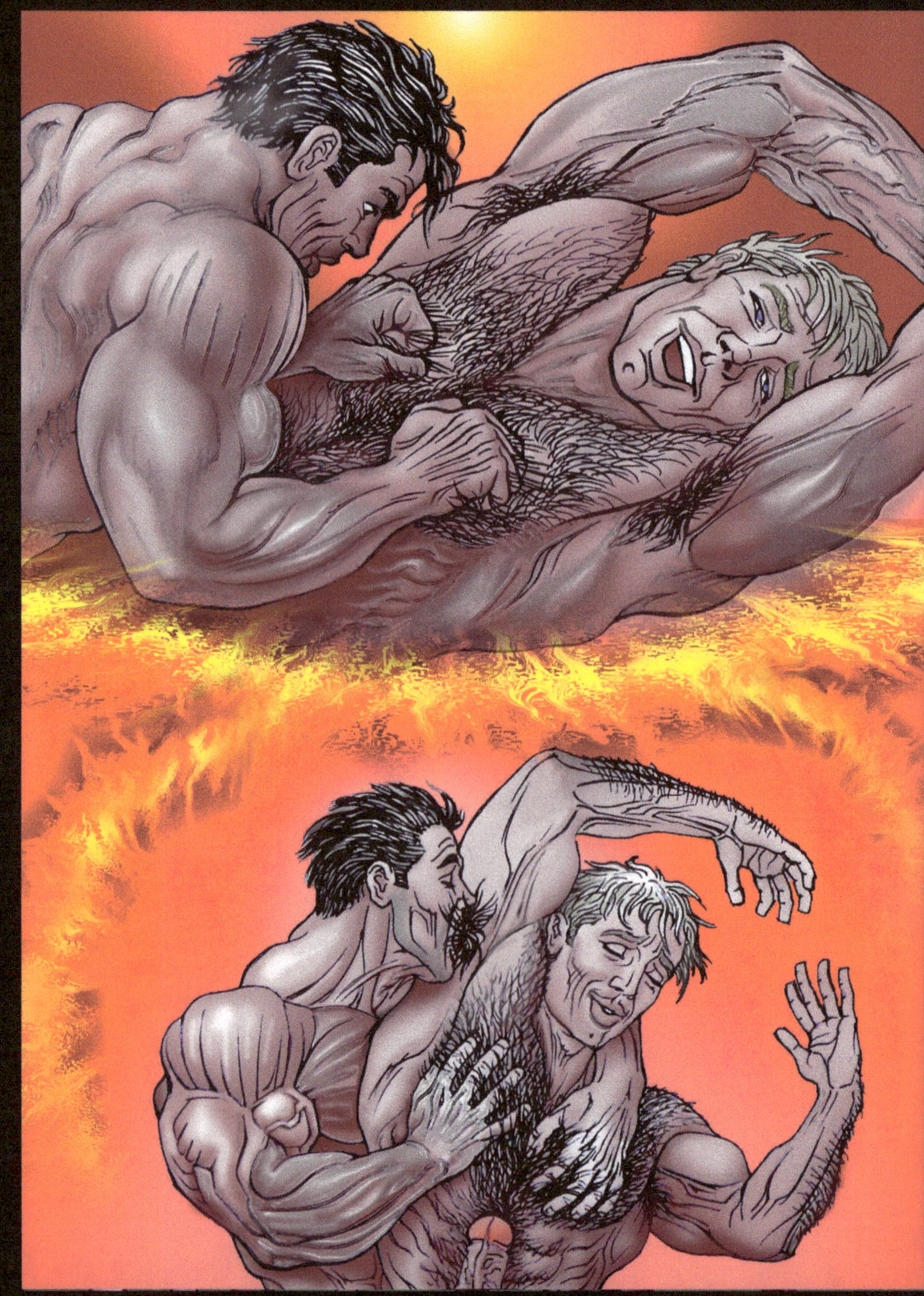

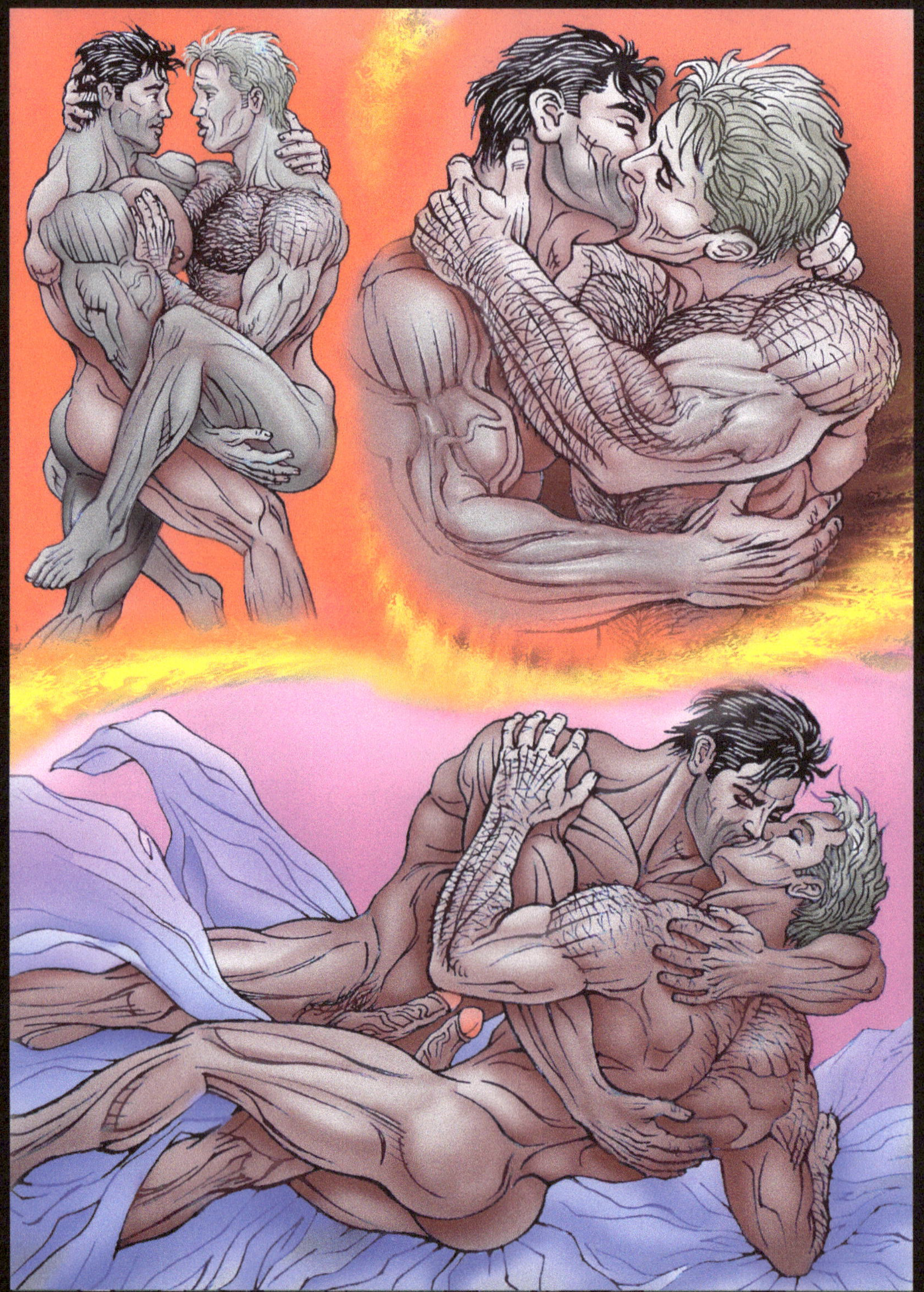

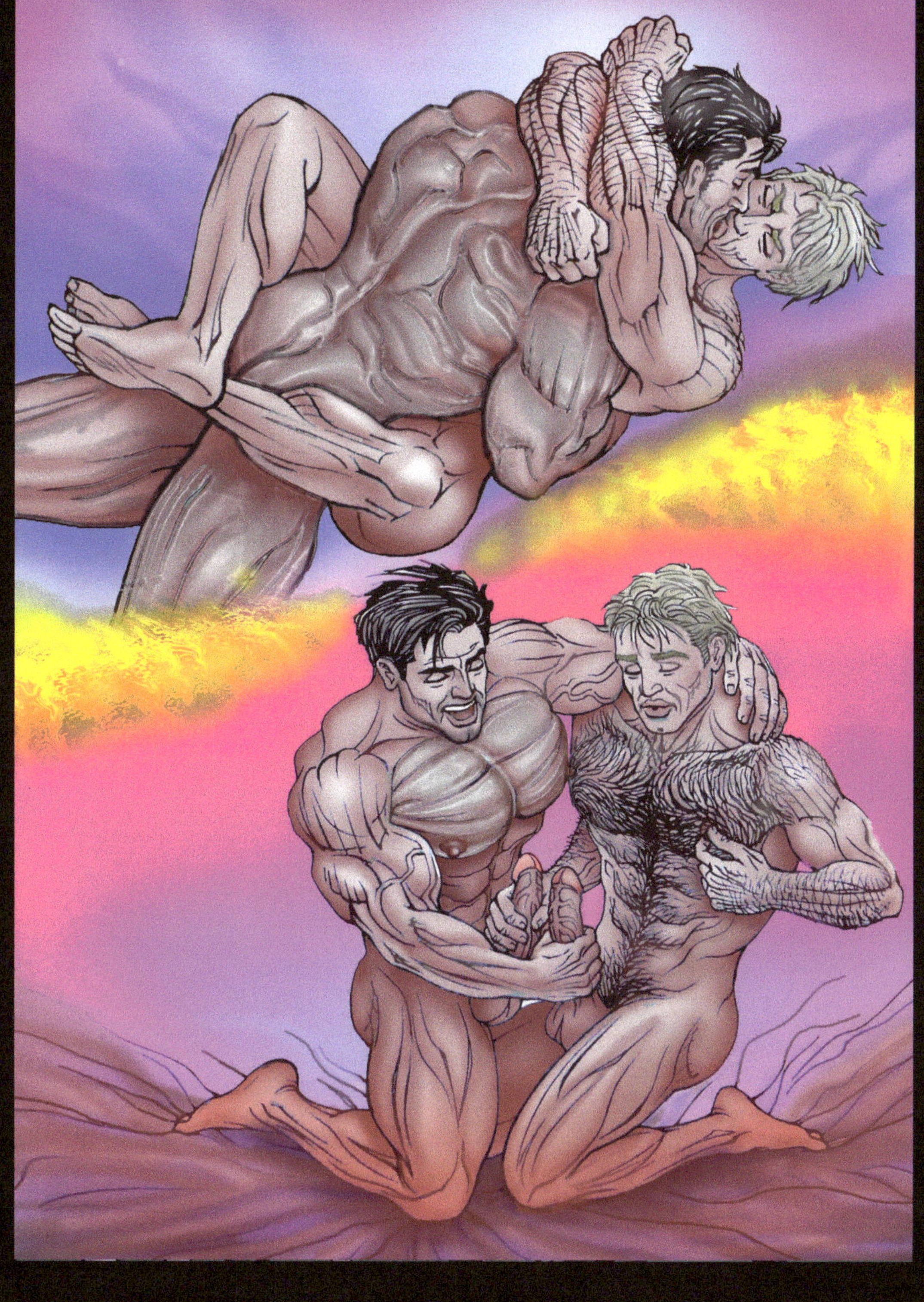

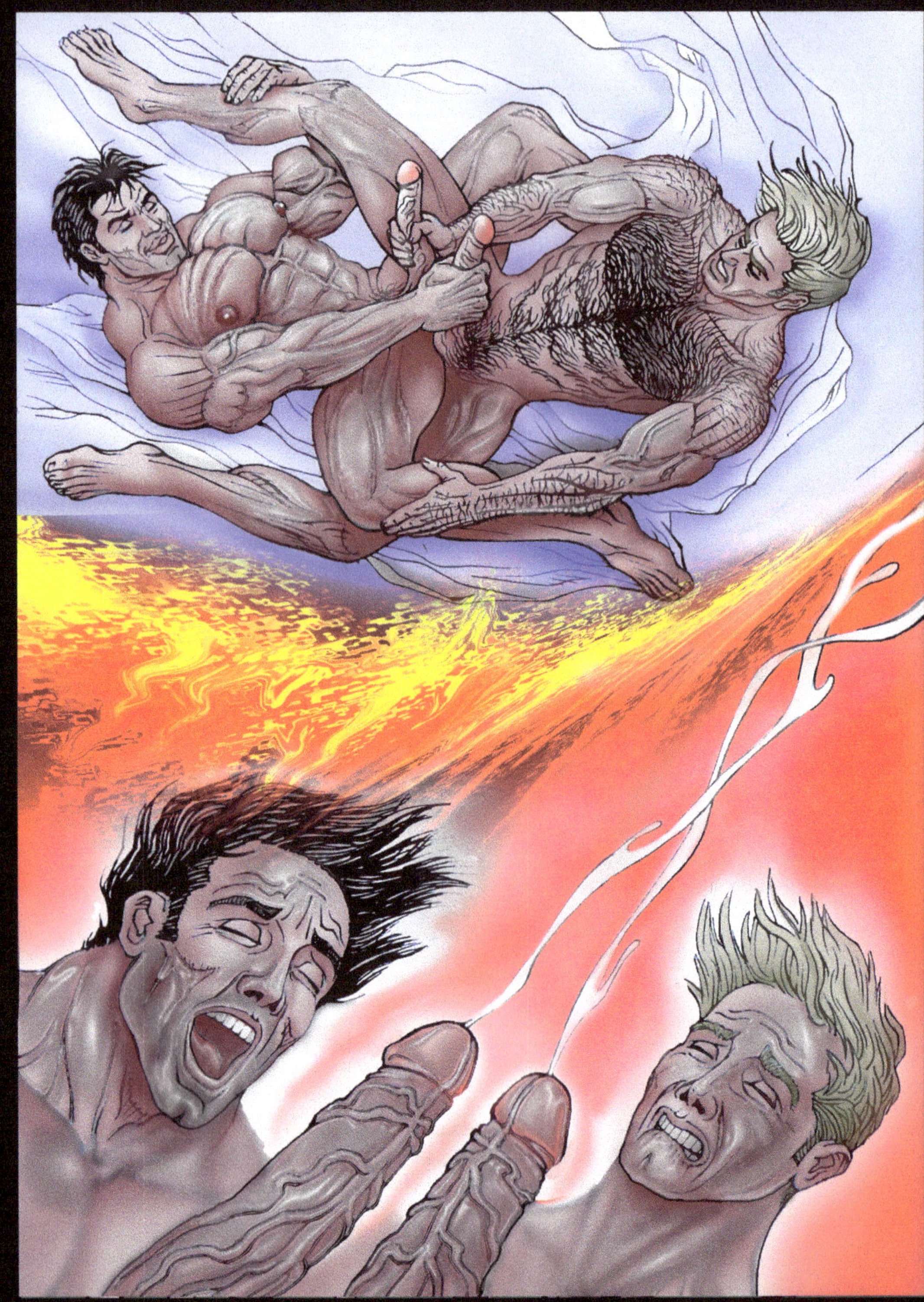

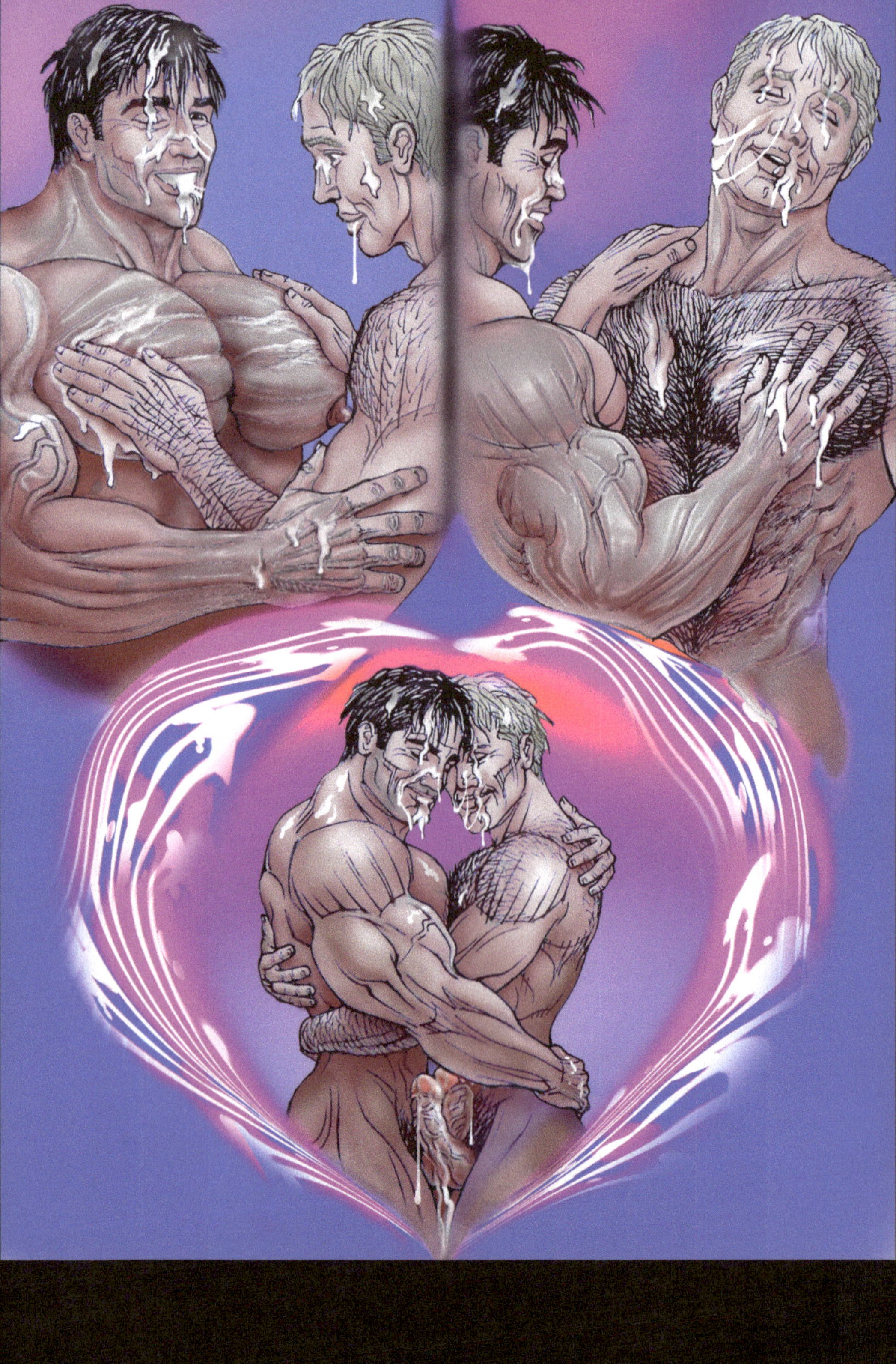

ВТО
ВАҀЕЛН
МОСК

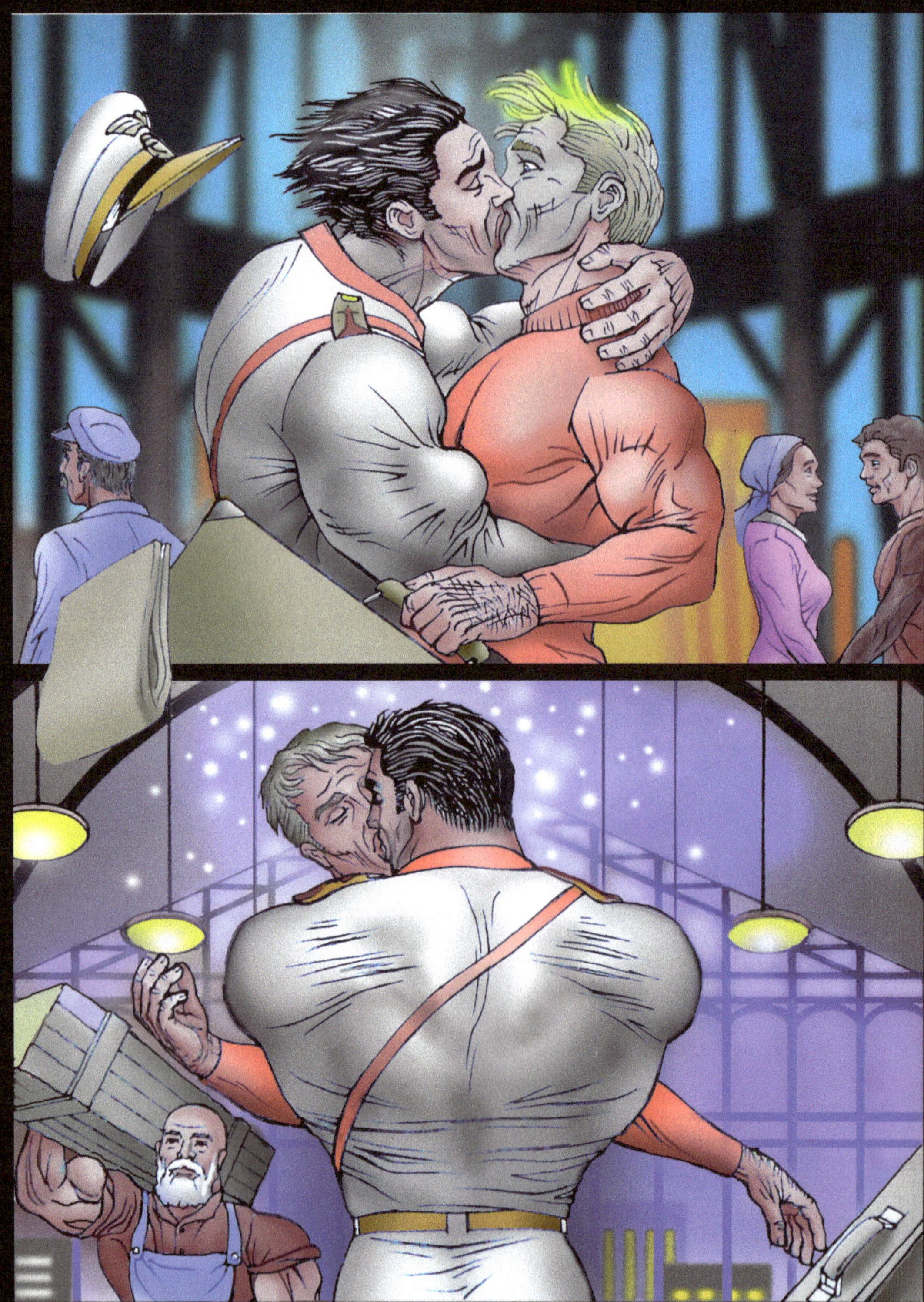

BERLINER
MAUER
1961 - 1989
THE END

script/art direction: Dale Lazarov
linework/colors: Enrique Nieto

About The Authors:

<u>Dale Lazarov</u> is known as The Father of American Bara Comics and The Stan Lee of Gay as the writer, art director and licensor of Sticky Graphic Novels. Sticky Graphic Novels are wordless, gay character-based, sex-positive graphic novels for an international audience that are considered "a joyous expression of male/male sexuality that, while erotic, is neither grubby nor tasteless" (*The Novel Approach*). Since 2006, he has collaborated on 16 hardcover Sticky Graphic Novels and 40 digital editions with distinctive and evocative gay comics artists from around the globe. In his secret identity, he is Aldo Alvarez, Ph.D., and lives in Chicago.

<u>Enrique Nieto</u> has always loved drawing the human body in action. Because of his admiration for artists such as Burne Hogarth, Joe Jusko, Frank Frazetta and many others, he had to dedicate himself to working on comics and illustration. It was difficult to find these kind of commissions in Spain and even in Europe, so he found work in American with Charlton Comics. In the Seventies, he illustrated many romantic, horror and adventure comics, preferring the latter two genres. Then he found an artists' representative in Europe and produced fantasy images for posters, book covers, puzzles, and other merchandise. In 2017, he began collaborating with Dale Lazarov on COMRADES.